My "k" Sound Box®

WRITTEN BY JANE BELK MONCURE • ILLUSTRATED BY REBECCA THORNBURGH

Published by The Child's World®
1980 Lookout Drive • Mankato, MN 56003-1705
800-599-READ • www.childsworld.com

ISBN HARDCOVER: 9781503823143
ISBN PAPERBACK: 9781503831360
LCCN: 2017960360

Printed in the United States of America
PA02430

A NOTE TO PARENTS AND EDUCATORS:

Magic moon machines and five fat frogs are just a few of the fun things you can share with children by reading books with them. Reading aloud helps children in so many ways! It introduces them to new words, motivates them to develop their own reading skills, and expands their attention span and listening abilities. So it's important to find time each day to share a book or two . . . or three!

As you read with young children, you can help develop their understanding of how print works by talking about the parts of the book—the cover, the title, the illustrations, and the words that tell the story. As you read, use your finger to point to each word, modeling a gentle sweep from left to right.

Simple word games help develop important prereading skills, including an understanding of rhyme and alliteration (when words share the same beginning sound, such as "six" and "sand"). Try playing with words from a book you've just shared: "What other words start with the same sound as moon?" "Cat and hat, do those words rhyme?" The possibilities are endless—and so are the rewards!

My "k" Sound Box®

Little  had a box. "I will find things that begin with my **k** sound," he said. "I will put them into my sound box."

"But first, I will be a  king."

So he dressed up like a  king.

Then Little went for a walk. He found a koala.

Did he put the koala into his box? He did.

Next, Little  found kingbirds.

Did he put the kingbirds into his box? He did.

Then Little found a kitten.

"Kitty, kitty," he called.

Lots and lots of kittens came from everywhere!

Little  tried to put the kittens into the  box. But the kingbirds did not like it.

Do you know why? What could Little  do?

He found a kangaroo. The

kangaroo had a big pocket.

Little  put all the kittens into the pocket.

"A  king can do anything!" said Little  .

So he played the kettledrum.

Then he put it into the box.

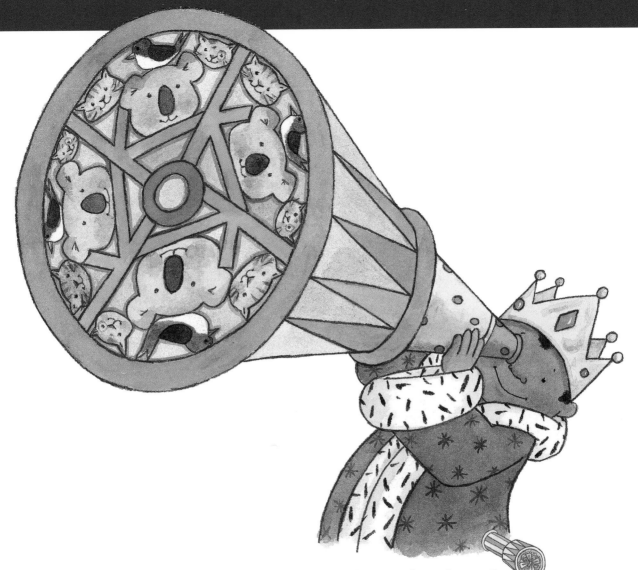

Next, he looked through a kaleidoscope.

Here is what he saw.

He put the kaleidoscope into the box, too.

Then Little  found kites, lots and lots of kites.

"I will fly a  kite," he said.

But the wind blew the 🪁 kite away.

The kingbirds flew after the  kite.

The kittens kicked the kangaroo.

The kangaroo sneezed—"Kerchoo!"—and blew

everything into a kindergarten classroom.

My, what fun the kids had!

Little 's Word List

kaleidoscope

kids

kite

kangaroo

kindergarten

kitten

kettledrum

king

koala

kingbird

Other Words with Little

kayak

kettle

kiss

keg

key

kitchen

ketchup

kimono

kiwi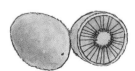

More to Do!

Little  found lots and lots of kites. You can make your own kite to fly. Follow the simple instructions below to make a diamond kite. Be sure to have an adult help you!

What you need:

- string or twine
- tape or glue
- 1 piece of heavy-duty paper, about 4 feet by 4 feet
- 1 thin wooden dowel that is 4 feet long
- 1 thin wooden dowel that is 3½ feet long
- markers, crayons, stickers, and paint for decorations
- scissors

Directions:

1. Cross the two dowels against each other to make a lowercase t. Wrap some string around the area where the dowels cross. Add a little glue to keep everything in place. Let this dry.

2. Have an adult cut a notch at each end of both dowels. Be sure the notches are deep enough so the string will fit into them.

3. Use your scissors to cut a piece of string that is long enough to stretch all the way around the kite frame.

4. Fasten the string to the top notch. Make a loop of string at the top. Now stretch the string to the next dowel's notch, and then the next. When you reach the top dowel again (where you started), wrap the string around a few times and tie a knot. Cut off any extra string. The string should be tight, but it shouldn't cause your dowels to bend.

5. Lay the paper flat and place the kite frame on top. Cut around the frame, leaving about an inch of paper left over on all sides. Fold these edges over the frame and tape or glue them down. The paper should be tight.

6. Cut another piece of string. Tie one end to the loop at the top. Tie the other end to the bottom of the kite. Tie another small loop just above the place where the two dowels cross. This is the kite's bridle. Attach your flying line to the bridle.

7. Decorate your kite. Now have fun flying it!

About the Author

Best-selling author Jane Belk Moncure (1926–2013) wrote more than 300 books throughout her teaching and writing career. After earning a master's degree in early childhood education from Columbia University, she became one of the pioneers in that field. In 1956, she helped form the Virginia Association for Early Childhood Education, which established the first statewide standards for teachers of young children.

Inspired by her work in the classroom, Mrs. Moncure's books became standards in primary education, and her name was recognized across the country. Her success was reflected not only in her books' popularity with parents, children, and educators, but also by numerous awards, including the 1984 C. S. Lewis Gold Medal Award.

About the Illustrator

Rebecca Thornburgh lives in a pleasantly spooky old house in Philadelphia. If she's not at her drawing table, she's reading—or singing with her band, called Reckless Amateurs. Rebecca has one husband, two daughters, and two silly dogs.